EMMA SAYS GOODBYE

EMMA SAYS GOODBYE

A Child's Guide: Bereavement

By Carolyn Nystrom
Illustrated by Annabel Large

A LION BOOK

For Sheri and her little one

Text copyright © 1990 Carolyn Nystrom
This illustrated edition © 1990 Lion Publishing

The author asserts the moral right
to be identified as the author of this work

Published by
Lion Publishing plc
Sandy Lane West, Oxford, England
ISBN 0 7459 2759 9
Albatross Books Pty Ltd
PO Box 320, Sutherland, NSW 2232, Australia
ISBN 0 7324 0794 X

First edition 1990
This paperback edition 1993

10 9 8 7 6 5 4 3 2 1

A catalogue record for this book is available
from the British Library

Printed and bound in Singapore

'Ouch!' squeaked Emma, as she jerked her finger
away from an offending pin in her square of
patchwork quilt.

'Here, try this.' Auntie Sue grinned and waved a
thimble in Emma's direction. 'It's a bit hard to get
used to, but it does save sore fingers.'

Emma studied the angle of the thimble on Auntie
Sue's right index finger, then slipped one on her own.

Making a quilt together had been Auntie Sue's
idea, and Emma thought it was a good one. But then
Emma liked most of Auntie Sue's ideas.

Pictures from their past flashed through Emma's mind. She scrambled across the sofa between them, dropping scraps of quilt on the way, to give Auntie Sue a hug.

'I love you, Auntie Sue,' she said. 'I'm glad you came to live with us. You're my favouritest aunt.'

'I love you too.' Auntie Sue laughed as she took Emma in her arms. 'But I don't know that "favourite aunt" is much of a compliment. I'm the only one you have. Your family seems to go in for uncles.'

Emma gathered up her quilt scraps and went back to her pictures of the past.

'Do you remember the time we celebrated the last day of term? We both turned cartwheels all over the front lawn.'

'The look on the postman's face—' Auntie Sue said.

They laughed together, remembering his surprised expression.

'And how about the time last summer when Matt was washing his new car and we leaned out of my bedroom window and dropped water balloons on him?'

'Your brother came after us both with the hose,' Auntie Sue chuckled.

'I hope you stay with us for ever, Auntie Sue,'
Emma said. 'Do you have to go back to work soon?'
    Auntie Sue bit her lip. 'I'm not sure,' she said
slowly. 'There's a lot I don't know just now.'
    Emma and her aunt sat quietly for a few minutes,
their needles busy with pastel bits of cloth. The
colours echoed the apple-blossom pink, soft violet,
and pale yellow of the spring outdoors, whispering at
their window.

But Emma did not see spring just then. In her mind she saw pictures of Auntie Sue from the past few weeks: doctors' appointments, tests, X-ray reports, white-uniformed nurses, visits to the doctor and hospital, and finally the short journey home—to get well.

'I'll have to get a lot stronger before I can climb telegraph poles and mend wires again,' Auntie Sue sighed.

Emma bent over her quilt block of spring pastels. She fastened a pale yellow triangle to one end of a sky blue rectangle, then turned the rectangle and stitched a second yellow triangle at the other end.

She and Auntie Sue had drawn the pattern for an eight-block quilt. Each of them would make four blocks—one for each season of the year. Then they would bind the eight blocks together with coloured patchwork squares from all the seasons. Finally, once the batting and lining were in place, they would put tiny, tiny stitches around the edge of each quilt piece to make it stand out from the rest.

Auntie Sue broke the silence. 'What does this square make you think of?' she asked.

Emma squeezed her lips together, turned her square from one side to the other and squinted at it.

'I'm not sure,' she said. 'From this side, it looks like the spade Mum used yesterday to dig holes for her new rose bushes—except that it has a point on the other end instead of a handle. But when I turn it this way, it looks like two oars for a boat.'

'A boat in a rushing river,' Auntie Sue said. 'I'd like to jump right in.'

'What does your square make you think of?' Emma returned the question.

'I was thinking of the bar and two triangles as an arrow that shoots two ways,' Auntie Sue said thoughtfully. 'One end points to heaven, and the other points to earth.'

12

Emma wondered why Auntie Sue had her mind on
heaven just then, but she couldn't think of a good
way to ask.

Summer did not start well at Emma's house. Auntie Sue went every day to the hospital for medicine. Her doctor hoped this 'chemotherapy' would kill the cancer cells in her body. But he warned her that the medicine would make her feel sick because it would kill good body cells too.

Auntie Sue lay on the sofa every afternoon. Sometimes Emma brushed her aunt's hair. Sometimes they watched TV together. Sometimes they read. And sometimes Emma got tired of being with a sick person all the time—even Auntie Sue. So she went away and played with her friends.

Each week Auntie Sue seemed to take less space as her body got thinner and thinner. Often she felt sick most of the day. By evening she could keep some soft food down, but in the morning she went back to the hospital for more medicine. Then the sick feelings would start all over again.

One frightening day, Auntie Sue's curly brown hair fell out in great clumps across the sofa cushions. Emma saw tears in her aunt's eyes as she swept the curls into the waste-paper basket. Then Auntie Sue walked slowly to her room and came back with a wig that she and Emma's mum had bought early in the summer—just in case.

On evenings when Auntie Sue did not feel well enough to eat at the table, Emma's family brought their food on trays to eat with her. Before their meal, they all paused to thank God for their food, as they always did. The one who said grace also asked God to help Auntie Sue get well.

At the end of the meal, if Auntie Sue felt specially bad, they all held hands in a circle with her and sang. Sometimes they sang 'Praise God from whom all blessings flow.' And sometimes, instead of singing, Mum or Dad would read a Psalm from the Bible.

It was a long seven weeks, but the chemotherapy did its work. Tests showed that Auntie Sue's blood was getting back to normal. She began to eat and laugh again. Even her hair grew back—in fuzzy tufts, like a boy's crew cut.

One bright blue August day Auntie Sue and Emma hired a canoe and paddled down a stream overhung by willows. Auntie Sue sat in front, and Emma steered from behind.

'In! Out!' Auntie Sue called as they dipped their paddles in unison, first to one side and then the other. Emma watched a willow branch brush Auntie Sue's thin white shoulder and remembered last summer, when Auntie Sue glowed with the dark tan and strong muscles of a telephone line engineer.

What about next summer? Emma wondered. Will Auntie Sue be healthy and strong and working again? Or will she . . . ?

No, of course not, Emma's thoughts objected. The doctor is working hard. And God won't let her die . . . not if we keep asking him to make her well.

Just then a screech from the front of the canoe brought Emma back to the present.

'Hey, give that back!' Auntie Sue shouted to a low-hanging branch.

Her wig waved defiantly from a sturdy twig as the summer breeze ruffled her short tufts of hair, and the current carried them downstream.

Emma and her aunt turned the canoe round. Twice they nearly got stuck in the bank, and once Emma jumped into the shallow water to keep the canoe from overturning. Finally they made it back to the tree.

Auntie Sue grabbed the wig from the branch, shook a scolding finger at the tree, and jammed the wig on her head—sideways, just to be silly.

Emma laughed until her sides hurt.

That evening, lightning crackled at their living-
room windows, while thunder crashed overhead.
Emma opened the curtains so that she and Auntie Sue
could watch as jagged streaks of lightning sawed
through boiling clouds. Emma rested her head on her
aunt's shoulder and felt safe. The violence outside
contrasted with the warm dry quiet of the living-
room. Gradually the intervals between flash and
rumble grew longer. Then torrents of rain lashed
against the window, blotting out their view of the sky.

Auntie Sue picked up quilt scraps as Emma turned on a lamp. This time they were stitching zigzag strips of poppy red on brilliant summer sky blue. Apple-green triangles braced the corners.

Emma traced the red edges with her needle. 'It looks like lightning,' she said. 'Except that it's the wrong colour. I wonder if lightning is ever red.'

'I don't think so,' answered her aunt. 'Maybe with the right kind of clouds or haze . . .' she continued doubtfully. 'But it reminds me of lightning too.'

They listened to the pounding rain.

'Lightning really does cut through the sky, doesn't it,' Emma said, remembering her science class. 'I think that's what makes the thunder—the air slamming back together after the lightning slices it apart.'

'Something like that,' murmured Auntie Sue. 'This zigzag lightning piece reminds me of a gap that slices like lightning between people.'

'Like when they get so cross with each other they won't talk?' Emma asked.

'Yes,' Auntie Sue replied. 'Or when they move far away from each other and can't be together any more.'

Emma and her aunt stitched silently for a moment. 'Or when they die,' Emma murmured softly.

But Auntie Sue didn't hear.

As summer with all its energy gave way to autumn, Emma saw her aunt's energy lag too. First she saw small changes, like the dark circles under her eyes in the mornings. Her footsteps on the wood floors sounded slow and shuffling, and she seemed to eat even less.

Emma returned to school, Matt went off to college—and Auntie Sue went back to the hospital. The cancer had returned. While Emma worked at fractions and long division, Auntie Sue had X-rays and blood tests.

Soon Auntie Sue was back home. Once again she spent most of her day on the living-room sofa, and once again she travelled every day to the hospital— this time for radiation therapy. Auntie Sue explained that machines sent X-rays into her body to try to burn up the cancer cells. The X-rays also burned her skin and made it red and sore. The X-rays seemed to burn up her energy too; she felt more tired than ever.

Emma's mum gave up her job, so that she could be at home with Auntie Sue all the time.

One crisp October day, Emma scuffed home from school through gold and crimson leaves layered ankle deep on the pavement. Everything felt brittle—the crunch of leaves swishing by her legs, the cool bite in the steel blue air, the snap in the tight red skin of the apple left from lunch in her jacket pocket.

As she came near to her house, Emma slowed her steps. She looked up at the porch, sagging slightly under the weight of its roof, and she felt her shoulders sag. Last spring she would have leapt up the porch steps, two at a time, but today she stopped, shuffled the leaves with her feet, pulled out the apple and began a private afternoon snack.

Finally, apple core in hand, she entered the front door. Her whole house smelt sick, as she knew it would. Even Mum's homemade vegetable soup, simmering on the stove, couldn't drive the smell away.

Emma dumped her apple core in the bin, then swept the half-empty baby-food jars and soggy paper cups of ice water from the worktop. That was Auntie Sue's lunch!

'How is she today?' she asked her mother, who had just appeared in the doorway.

'About the same,' came the wooden reply.

'When is she going to get better?' Emma sighed. 'I'm tired of Auntie Sue being sick.'

Mum didn't answer.

Emma saw that her mother's tired grey eyes didn't quite meet hers. Instead they seemed to look at a point somewhere behind her left shoulder.

Emma felt her mouth go dry. 'She's not going to get well, is she, Mum?' A shudder rocked her whole body. 'Auntie Sue is going to die!'

Mum held her close and stroked her hair until her shaking stopped.

'Does she know?' Emma whispered.

Mum nodded.

'Is it all right if I talk to her about it?'

'I think that would be good for both of you,' Mum agreed.

That evening Emma and her aunt worked once
again at their quilt. This time they were not in the
living-room. Auntie Sue sat propped up in her bed
with pillows all around, so that nothing hard would
touch her sensitive skin. Mum had fastened bags onto
the side of the bed to hold the things Auntie Sue
needed. Her quilt scraps lay in a basket on the floor.
The curtains were open, even though it was nearly
dark, because Auntie Sue liked to watch the last hint
of twilight.

They stitched quietly for a while, working on the
autumn shades of gold and crimson and olive green.
In the middle of their square was a large, brown,
roughly oval shape. Emma, in a whimsical moment,
had made the pattern by tracing round one of her

32

father's shoes. Auntie Sue had liked its shape, and so they had designed it into their autumn quilt square.

Emma felt a lump in her throat getting bigger and bigger, until she could hardly swallow at all.

Finally she said, 'Auntie Sue, you're not getting better, are you?'

'No, I'm not.'

'And you aren't ever going to get well and go back to work?'

'No.'

'Auntie Sue, I love you.' Emma put her arms round her aunt's thin shoulders and felt her short bristly hair against her face.

'Last spring, I thought you'd come here to live with us,' she said. 'But you didn't. You came here to die.'

'How could God let you die?' Emma asked. 'We've asked him every day to make you better.'

Auntie Sue was quiet for a moment. Then she spoke slowly. 'I know that God hears our prayers. And I know that he loves us. But he doesn't always give us what we ask—even when it is as important as life. I don't know why.'

Emma felt anger creep up the back of her neck: anger at her parents for bringing Auntie Sue into her quiet healthy home, anger at Auntie Sue for being sick, anger at the doctors for not making her well, and even anger at God—a God who was supposed to love them, but who was going to let Auntie Sue die anyway.

Auntie Sue seemed to mirror her thoughts.

'Sometimes I look at this skinny, sick body of mine, and I get mad,' she said. 'This isn't the me I want to be!' She slapped her thin leg. 'I don't know why God is letting this happen to me, but I know he's promised the people who love him that he'll never leave them alone. I think of him when I look at that big footprint on our quilt. No matter what happens, God keeps right on walking with me. So, even when I die, I won't die alone.'

Autumn rustled into winter. Matt came home from college for Christmas. Emma watched his eyes widen when he saw Auntie Sue's thin, sick body propped up in a hospital bed in her room. He kissed Auntie Sue lightly on the cheek, touched her cropped hair, and then whirled out, closing the door to his own room. Usually when Matt was at home the house was full of music and friends. But this year Matt went away a lot. And when he played music it was soft guitar, late at night alone in his room. Emma missed him.

Christmas Day dawned grey and damp-cold. By ten o'clock lacy flakes of snow drifted from the sky, etching the black trees with white. A fire crackled through apple logs in the fireplace. On the stereo a choir sang Handel's *Messiah* while the family opened gifts. Everything seemed slower and quieter this year. For one thing, Auntie Sue wasn't scrambling around the room trying to see all the presents at once. Instead, she sat, small and frail, propped in a wheelchair. But she had done her shopping. Auntie Sue gave Emma a bright green sweater she'd picked out in a catalogue.

Emma had thought a long time about what to give Auntie Sue. (What *do* you give a person who is dying?) Finally she chose a large picture book of a

story Auntie Sue had read to her when she was little.
Auntie Sue's smile showed that she remembered.
They would read it again.

'Hallelujah!' rang out trumpets, strings and voices on the stereo.

'The kingdom of this world is become the kingdom of our Lord, and of his Christ: and he shall reign for ever and ever.'

'What this party needs is a little dancing,' said Auntie Sue. 'And that is just the kind of music to dance to. I'm not quite up to it at the moment, but give me some time.' She wiggled expectantly in her wheelchair. 'One of these days I'm going to be as alive as a new colt, and I'm going to dance around Jesus.'

It was hard not to smile, Auntie Sue seemed so eager. Emma sprang up. 'Why not get started now?' she

said. She swung her new green sweater across her
shoulders and whirled round the living-room, stooping
every now and then to touch Auntie Sue, who
clapped her hands in time to the music.

The trumpets soared higher and higher as the
chorus sang the final words—'King of Kings, and Lord
of Lords, Hallelujah!'

January turned bitter cold. Long blue shadows of bare trees crept across the snow. A hospice worker came each day to help with Auntie Sue's medicines and bath. An oxygen cylinder stood near the bed to ease her breathing when she needed it. Emma came each day after school to her aunt's room. Each day Auntie Sue seemed weaker.

The quilt came out only once in January. One pale afternoon, they started on the winter block—a large white circle edged with greys and black. Auntie Sue leaned on one bony elbow and tried to stitch with the other hand, but the position made breathing hard. She stopped sewing for a moment to rest.

'That circle is like life, Emma,' she said. 'You put your needle in at one point and you pick it up somewhere else. It never ends.'

Emma dropped her own square and met her aunt's eyes. 'Like when Jesus died,' Emma said, 'he came back to life?'

'Yes, and we will too,' her aunt said. 'People who love Jesus move from life here to life with him. Death doesn't end life. Life just begins again in heaven.'

Emma nodded. She felt her chin trembling. 'But I'll miss you terribly here,' she cried.

'I know,' her aunt replied.

Auntie Sue handed over her block. 'Here. You'll have to finish this.'

Then she leaned back on her pillows and began to breathe more easily.

The next morning, Emma heard hushed voices,
even before she opened her eyes. She stumbled into
her aunt's room. Mum and Dad were both there. The
oxygen machine was running. Auntie Sue's breathing
was fast and shallow. She stirred restlessly, but seemed
asleep.

Dad did not go to work that day, and Emma stayed
away from school. Mum called Matt at college. Mum
and Dad took it in turn to sit in Auntie Sue's room.
They held her thin hand and talked to her.
Sometimes she seemed to squeeze a hand in return,
but she didn't open her eyes.

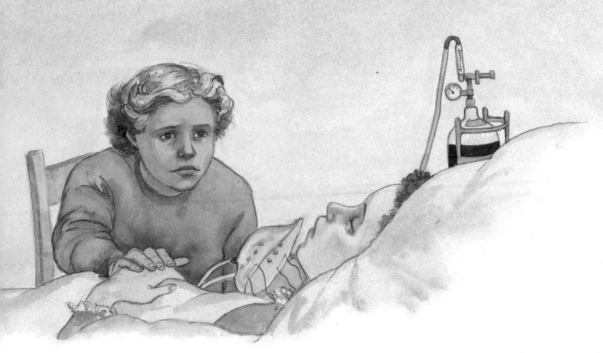

By late afternoon Auntie Sue's breathing got slower and slower. Emma and her parents stood together near the bed. Dad opened his Bible and began to read.

'For I am certain that nothing can separate us from God's love: neither death nor life . . . There is nothing in all creation that will ever be able to separate us from the love of God which is ours through Christ Jesus our Lord.'

While Dad was reading, Matt slipped into the room, guitar in hand. Softly he began to sing, 'Jesus loves me.' During the song, Emma saw her aunt search for one last breath—then stop. Her family held each other and cried.

Months later, spring sun warmed Emma's back as she spread her newly finished quilt on the shaded grass to dry. Mum had helped with the batting and lining and border. But Emma had quilt-stitched round the edges of each piece herself. Her stitches got smaller and more regular as she went along. By the end, she could hardly tell which pieces were Auntie Sue's and which were her own. The colours of the seasons, each with its own memories, blended into the background of green grass.

The cold of January blurred into the past. A house full of relatives, neighbours, and friends. A refrigerator packed with food brought by people who wanted to help. A coffin with a spray of flowers on top and Auntie Sue inside looking asleep in her long-sleeved blue silk dress. Friends standing in front of the coffin and crying. A funeral at church full of music and words from the Bible about living for ever in heaven with Jesus, where people play and sing and dance and work, and no one ever, ever cries.

A gaping hole in snow-edged cemetery ground. Auntie Sue's coffin lowered down inside and covered with cold chunks of black earth. The words of Jesus, read aloud: 'I am the resurrection and the life. He who believes in me will live, even though he dies.'

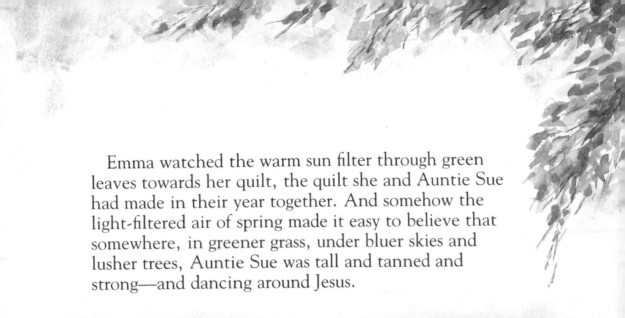

Emma watched the warm sun filter through green leaves towards her quilt, the quilt she and Auntie Sue had made in their year together. And somehow the light-filtered air of spring made it easy to believe that somewhere, in greener grass, under bluer skies and lusher trees, Auntie Sue was tall and tanned and strong—and dancing around Jesus.